# A Monster
## in the House

**Canadian Cataloguing in
Publication Data**

Tremblay, Carole, 1959-
(Véridique histoire de Destructotor. English)
A Monster in the House
Translation of: Véridique histoire de Destructotor.

ENGLISH TEXT: GABRIEL GAY HOMEL

ISBN 1-894363-46-9

I. Gay Homel, Gabriel II. Jolin, Dominique, 1964-
III. Title. IV. Title: Véridique histoire de Destructotor. English.

PS8589.R39428V4713 2000    jC843'.54    C00-900497-1
PZ7.T71924Mo 2000

Publisher: Dominique Payette
Series Editor: Lucie Papineau
Graphic Design: Primeau & Barey

Legal Deposit: 3rd Quarter 2000
Bibliothèque nationale du Québec
National Library of Canada

Printed in Canada
10 9 8 7 6 5 4 3 2

**Dominique & Friends**
Canada:
300 Arran Street, Saint Lambert,
Quebec, Canada, J4R 1K5
USA:
P.O. Box 800
Champlain, New York
12919
Tel: 1-888-228-1498
Fax: 1-888-782-1481
E-mail:
dominique.friends@editionsheritage.com

The publisher wishes to thank the Canada Council for its
support, as well as SODEC and Canadian Heritage.

*For Victor, Gabou and Stéphane –*
*every which way*

**Carole Tremblay · Dominique Jolin**

# A Monster
## in the House

When Victor was born,
everyone thought he was wonderful.
"What a nice baby!"
"He looks just like his father."
"With his mother's nose."
"And his grandfather's gums."
"He'll look like his sister. She has
her grandmother's ears and
Uncle Tom's toes!"

I'm his sister. Right away, I saw that Victor was a monster.

But nobody listened to me. Everyone said
I was jealous, and that was normal.
Only later on did they admit I was right.

Back then, it was
the good old days;
Victor couldn't even hold
a toy in his little hands.
All he could do
was scream.

And when I say scream,
I mean *scream*.

Even our neighbours
on the eighth floor had
to wear earplugs.

My Dad, who
is a considerate man,
gave them out.

But those good days didn't last long.

The Monster was almost four months
old when he got hold of his first toy. An innocent
pink and baby-blue rattle that belonged to me
when I wore diapers.

The toy didn't last ten minutes
in the Monster's hands.

After destroying Mom's glasses with the punch
of the century, Victor threw the rattle in the
big pot filled with boiling soup.

After that, things went from bad to worse. We couldn't
walk through the room where the Monster was without
getting pelted with projectiles. Victor threw everything
he could get his hands on. When there wasn't anything left,
he would get undressed and throw his clothes.
The worst time was when I got hit by
a diaper right in the face.

Dad, who is a careful man,
made us special helmets for our protection.

One day, the Monster began to eat. I was afraid
Mom wouldn't survive the ordeal. Not one wall wasn't
covered with baby food after his dinner.

Dad, who is a practical man, renovated the kitchen.
He installed giant windshield wipers on every wall,
and hoses to clean them after every meal.

When my little brother
learned to crawl, I began having
nightmares. What if he crawled
into my room at night and began to
demolish everything? I asked
Mom to buy some chains and
locks for my room.

At first, she didn't want to.
But when Victor stuck holes in
my pillow with my multicoloured pen,
she had to admit that a lock
wouldn't be a bad idea after all.

Dad, who is a skilled handyman,
helped protect me.

By the time the Monster was eight months old, he had
destroyed three-quarters of his toys. Objects that had great
sentimental and historical value because I had played
with them when I was a baby.

The rubber ducky
melted on the radiator.

The plush hippopotamus
lost its eyes and ears.

The wooden clown was turned into a construction set.

Dad, who is a sensible man, decided that fragile toys were not for him. I sorted through the toychest and left only the toughest ones for him.

Since there weren't many, Mom let him play with the kitchen utensils.

Bad idea, a very bad idea. The Monster
started banging away with his new toys. He destroyed the
cupboard with the rolling pin. He shredded the armchair
with the cheese grater. Victor threw the strainer out
the window. It landed on Mrs. Gunn's head and it took
half an hour to get it out of her hair.

"Big problems call for big solutions!" declared
Dad, who is a man of many ideas. He put screens
on all the windows. He installed safes where
the cupboards had been.

Mom had to remember hundreds
of combinations just to put away the dishes.

When Victor was one year old, he learned to walk.
And worse – he learned to climb. Mom was losing
her voice because she was always screaming.
"Ahhhhhh! No, Victor, not that!"

Dad, who is a clever man, bought her a microphone
so she could save her vocal cords.

The day the little devil put Mom's wallet
in the blender, I thought she was going to have
a heart attack. Finally, I got mad.

I took Dad's fishing
net and caught Victor in it.

Dad, who is an intelligent man,
realized I had a good idea. He set traps
on the ceiling. When we pulled the rope,
the net would fall and catch the Monster.
Dad said he was going to perfect the
system with remote control.

When Victor was one-and-a-half years old, his favourite
game consisted of unrolling toilet paper all over the house.
Mom would let him do that. She laughed and said
he was playing mummy.

But when he threw a whole roll down
the toilet, then flushed it, and the bathroom flooded,
she didn't think that was so funny.

Dad, who is a good plumber, built a big drain
in the middle of the bathroom in case Victor decided
to flood the house again.

When the Monster was
two years old, he developed the bad
habit of dragging my parents' bed
down the staircase. Dad, who is handy
with tools, solved the problem
by nailing all the furniture
to the floor.

When Victor was three,
he was so strong he would
beat me at arm wrestling.
Mom would ask him to open
the jars of jam that were
stuck shut. And Dad got him
to carry his toolbox.

By the time Victor was four years old, he spoke perfect
English, and began to be less dangerous. Mom started thinking
we might live a normal life again. But then Dad, who is
an excellent worker, lost his job. We had to sell our house
because we didn't have enough money.
Mom was very upset.

"Who would buy a house with traps on the ceiling and windshield wipers on the walls?" But when the real-estate agent came to visit, he said the house was a masterpiece. "It's perfect for raising gorillas! What an extraordinary concept!"

Now Dad is making a fortune building houses
for gorillas, with Victor's help. He demolishes the walls
and ceilings, and Dad rebuilds them.

Victor has a lot of gorilla friends. Gorillas from
all around the world. We travel a lot because of Dad's job.
We have seen the four corners of the earth. And now
I hear they're going to build a gorilla house on Mars,
where scientists will carry out experiments.

I get along with my little brother,
now that he's older. And now that he's bigger,
he has stopped breaking things.

Well, almost…

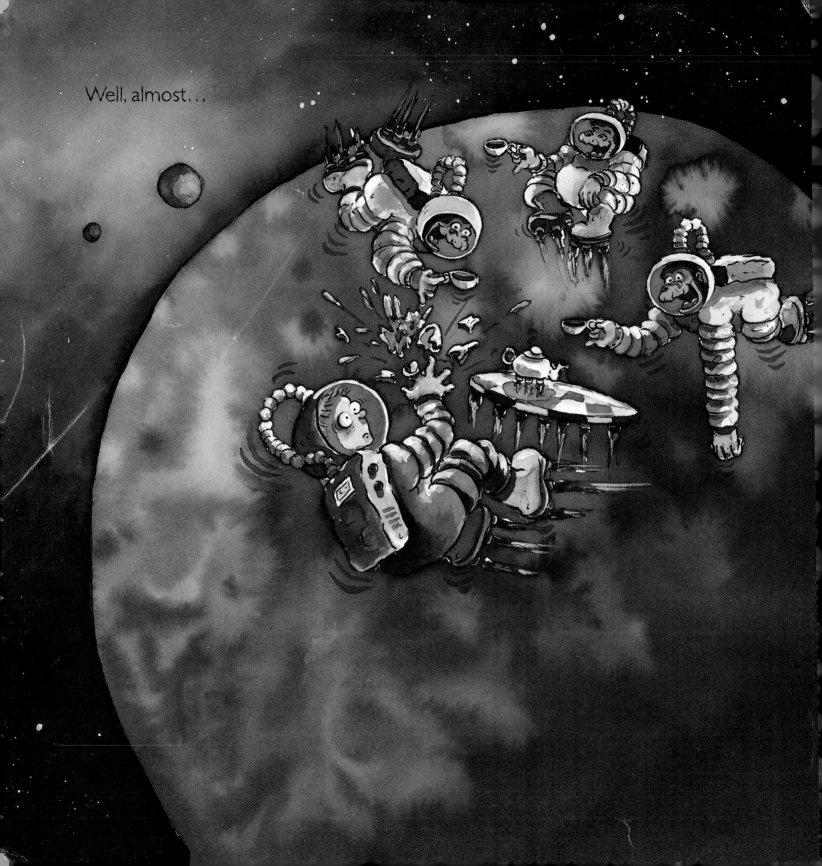